# KALEIDOSCOPE

# Galaxies

**Dan Elish**

 **Marshall Cavendish**
Benchmark
New York

Marshall Cavendish Benchmark
99 White Plains Road
Tarrytown, New York 10591-9001
www.marshallcavendish.us

Library of Congress Cataloging-in-Publication Data
Elish, Dan.
Galaxies / by Dan Elish.
p. cm. — (Kaleidoscope)
Includes bibliographical references and index.
ISBN-13: 978-0-7614-2047-7 (alk. paper)
ISBN-10: 0-7614-2047-9 (alk. paper)
1. Galaxies—Juvenile literature. 2. Milky Way—Juvenile literature. I. Title. II. Series: Kaleidoscope (Tarrytown, N.Y.)
QB857.3.E45 2006             523.1'12—dc22             2005017933

Editor: Marilyn Mark
Editorial Director: Michelle Bisson
Art Director: Anahid Hamparian
Series Designer: Adam Mietlowski

Photo Research by Anne Burns Images
Cover Photo by Corbis/Sygma

The photographs in this book are used with permission and through the courtesy of: *Corbis*: p. 1, 11 Myron Jay Dorf; p. 7, 19, 43 Bettman; p. 8 Reuters; p. 23 Sygma; p. 36 NASA/Roger Ressmeyer: p. 40 Sygma/Hamilton Karie *Science Photo Library*: p. 4 Mark Garlick; p. 12 Detlev Van Ravenswaay; p. 24 Space Telescope Science Institute/Nasa; p. 31 Celestial Image Co.; p. 39 Mehau Kulyk *Art Resource*: p. 15 Victoria & Albert Museum, London *Getty Images*: p. 16 *Photri-Microstock*: p. 20, 28, 35 *Nasa*: p. 27 *Photo Researchers Inc.*: p. 32 NOAO/AURA/NSF.

Printed in Malaysia

6 5 4 3 2 1

# Contents

The Big Bang     5

The Milky Way     9

Hubble's Galaxies     14

Galaxies Galore     29

Quasars     37

Are We Alone?     41


Glossary     44

Find Out More     46

Index     48

# The Big Bang

Imagine that there was no universe—that the Sun, stars, and planets did not exist. Then imagine that in one giant flash, all matter and energy came into being. This is how most *astronomers* think the universe was created. This theory is called the *Big Bang*. For millions of years after the Big Bang, the universe was incredibly hot. When it finally began to cool, matter separated into large clumps held together by *gravity* and then formed into systems of stars, dust, and gas. Each of these systems is called a *galaxy*.

*This artwork depicts the Big Bang, a scientific theory of how the universe came to be.*

For many years, scientists believed that there was only one galaxy in the universe, but recent research has shown that there are literally billions of galaxies, each with billions of stars.

*Three early astronomers, Aristotle (384-322 BCE), Ptolemy (85-165 CE), and Copernicus (1473-1543 CE) appear on the title page of Galileo Galilei's* Concerning the Two Chief World Systems, *published in 1635. Galileo agreed with Copernicus's theory that the Earth revolved around the Sun, which went against the widely accepted principles proposed by Aristotle and Ptolemy.*

DIALOGVS
# DE SYSTEMATE MVNDI,
Autore
GALILÆO GALILÆI LYNCEO,
SERENISSIMO
FERDINANDO II. HETRVR. MAGNO-DVCI
dicatus.

# The Milky Way

How big is a galaxy? Galaxies are so large that miles and kilometers are not big enough to measure them. Instead, astronomers use a unit called a *light-year*, which is the distance that light travels in a year. Light moves very fast, at a speed of 186,000 miles (about 299,337 kilometers) per second. The light from a star that is one light-year away travels through space for an entire year before it reaches the Earth!

*Galaxies come in all sizes and shapes. The warped, dusty disk of galaxy ESO 510-G13, seen here, shows an unusual twisted disk structure. This is unlike most spiral galaxies, which appear flat when viewed from this angle. This galaxy is 150 million light-years away from Earth.*

Nearly every star and planet that can be seen in the sky is part of Earth's home galaxy, the *Milky Way*. Measuring between 100,000 and 130,000 light-years in *diameter*, the Milky Way is home to some 200 billion stars. It is shaped like a disk with a bulge at its center, or a little bit like two fried eggs slapped back to back. Spirals of stars shoot out from its center. Stars on the Milky Way's edge are about five light-years away from one another. Near the center, the stars are about one hundred times closer together. In much the same way that planets *orbit*, or rotate around, the Sun, the stars in the Milky Way rotate around the center of the galaxy.

*This artwork depicts the Milky Way, Earth's home galaxy.*

Earth's Solar System is part of the Milky Way. It lies about 25,000 light-years from its center. It takes our Sun 225 million years to make a full rotation around the Milky Way.

*This illustration of the Solar System shows the planets' orbits as blue lines. In their order from the Sun, the planets are: Mercury, Venus, Earth, Mars, Jupiter, Saturn, Uranus, Neptune, and Pluto. The asteroid belt (rocks left over from the formation of the Solar System) is in the middle, and the Milky Way, Earth's galaxy, is seen in the background at the right.*

# Hubble's Galaxies

For many years scientists did not know a lot about our universe. In the mid-1500s, a man named Nicolas Copernicus published his idea that the rotating Earth orbited the Sun. In 1610 the astronomer Galileo used a telescope to see the moons of Jupiter and to chart individual stars in the Milky Way.

*The Copernican Solar System illustrates astronomer Nicolas Copernicus's theory that the Earth revolves around the Sun. This concept went against the beliefs of his time. Most people believed that the Earth was the center of the universe and that nothing existed beyond the universe. Today, Copernicus is considered one of the founders of modern astronomy.*

By the twentieth century, astronomers had figured out that there was one definite galaxy, the Milky Way. They also discovered that the sky was full of small clouds of light made of dust and gas called *nebulae*.

*This is the Eagle Nebula in an image released by NASA on April 25, 2005. It is one of the sharpest images Hubble has ever produced. These clouds of dust and gas will eventually form into new stars.*

In 1924 an astronomer named Edwin Hubble was the first to discover that the universe contained more than one galaxy. Hubble worked at the Mount Wilson Observatory in California. Studying photographs taken through a powerful telescope, Hubble first noticed star systems outside of our galaxy and concluded that there were nine galaxies in the universe. As a result of his research, Hubble was able to name and identify three different kinds of galaxies.

*Edwin Hubble guides a 48-inch telescope through a series of rehearsals before it is used in a sky survey. Hubble became the foremost astronomer of his day.*

A *spiral galaxy* is like our Milky Way. It is a collection of stars with a bulge at the center. This bulge is surrounded by spiral circles of younger stars. In a spiral galaxy new stars and solar systems keep forming as space dust and gas combine.

*This galaxy, M-74, has been called the "perfect spiral galaxy" because of its nearly ideal form. M-74 is believed to be home to about 100 billion stars, making it slightly smaller than our Milky Way.*

*Elliptical galaxies* are the largest. They contain up to a trillion stars. Shaped something like a football, elliptical galaxies have less dust and gas than spiral galaxies. As a result, they create fewer new stars. Some elliptical galaxies are thought to have been formed when two or three spiral galaxies collided in space.

*These Hubble telescope images, taken in 2001, show nearby galaxies. By viewing these galaxies in ultraviolet light, astronomers could compare their shapes with those of distant galaxies.*

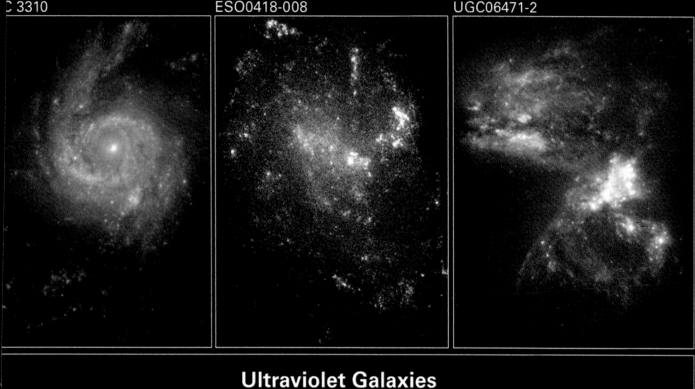

**Ultraviolet Galaxies**

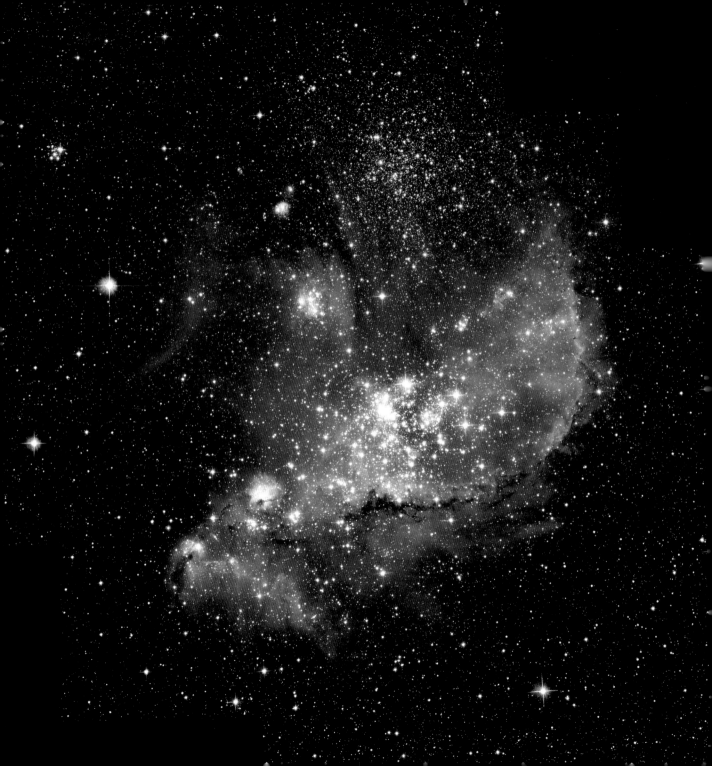

*Irregular galaxies* have no set pattern or structure. They contain a lot of dust and bright nebulae.

Today, astronomers classify two other types of galaxies as well. *Barred spirals* have a bar of stars that run across the middle of the galaxy. *Lenticular galaxies* are shaped like a lens and contain large amounts of dust, but not much gas.

*This nebula is part of the Small Magellanic Cloud, an irregular galaxy located about 200,000 light-years away from Earth.*

These discoveries would have assured Hubble's place as one of the twentieth century's greatest astronomers, but he had even more to contribute. At the time Hubble was conducting his research, a man named Milton Humason was working at the *observatory* as a janitor. In 1919 George Hale, the director of the observatory, recognized that Humason had great ability as a star-observer and promoted him to the scientific staff. Working together, Hubble and Humason made a startling new discovery. They found that the universe's galaxies were moving. Not only that, but the farther the galaxies were from Earth, the faster they moved. In other words, the universe was expanding, or growing larger.

*Hubble's and Humason's discovery seen at work: galaxy NGC 2207 and IC 2163 pass each other in a dramatic near collision.*

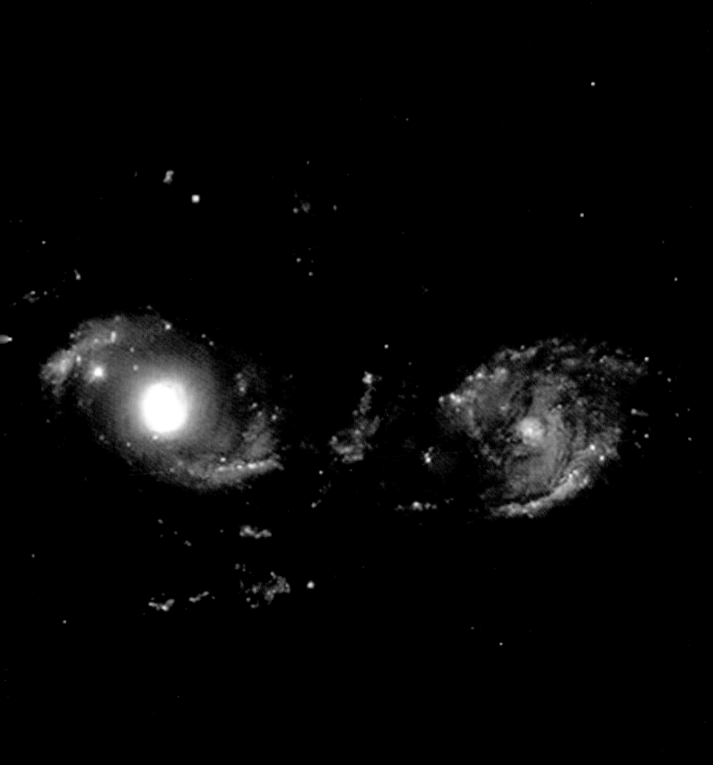

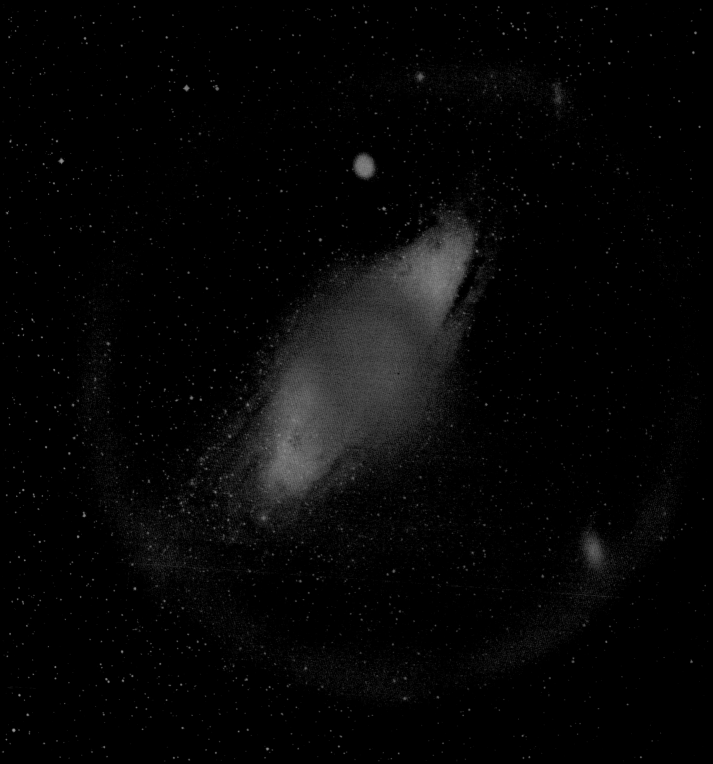

# Galaxies Galore

Though we now know that the universe is filled with billions of other galaxies, only three of them can be seen with the naked eye. In 964 CE, Persian astronomer As-Sufi became the first to identify an odd milky cluster in the northern part of the sky. It was not until the 1920s that Edwin Hubble proved that these stars made up their own galaxy called *Andromeda*. Located about 2.3 million light-years away, Andromeda is a spiral galaxy that contains almost 400 billion stars.

*This is the center of the Andromeda galaxy, our large neighboring galaxy. Astronomer As-Sufi called this galaxy "the Little Cloud" in his* Book of Fixed Stars.

The two other visible galaxies are the *Large Magellanic Cloud* and the *Small Magellanic Cloud*. They are both irregular galaxies that are smaller than the Milky Way. They are located about 200,000 light-years away and can be seen in the southern part of Earth's sky.

*This image shows the Large Magellanic Cloud, an irregular galaxy. Several pink nebulae are shown, including the Tarantula nebula (upper right), which is one of the largest and most powerful nebulae known.*

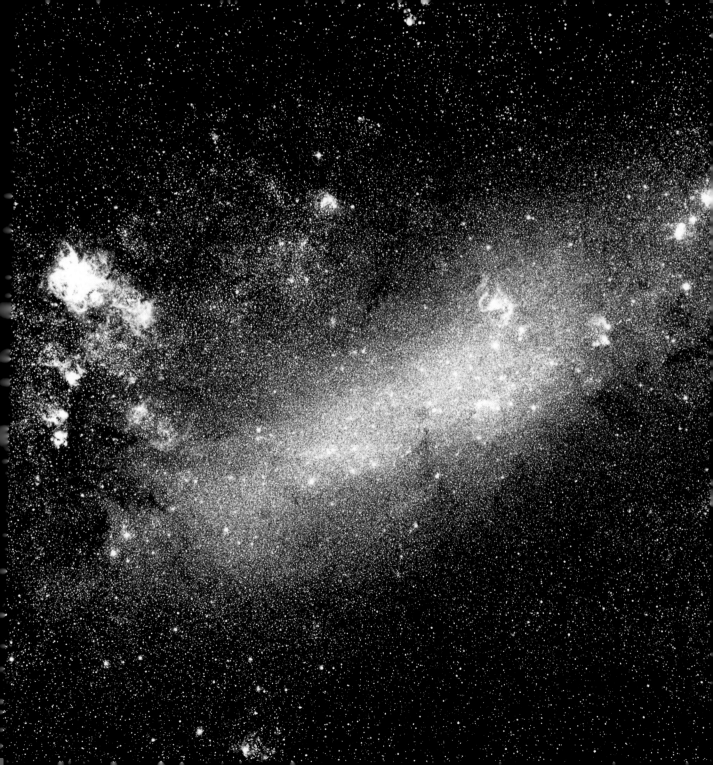

Though many light-years apart, these three galaxies are actually part of our own neighborhood in the universe. Some galaxies are loners, moving through the universe by themselves, but about 60 percent of all galaxies move in groups called *clusters*. The Milky Way, Andromeda, and the Large and Small Magellanic Clouds are part of a larger cluster called the *Local Group*. These thirty or so galaxies measure around 3 million light-years wide. Each galaxy in this cluster moves on its own. At the same time, all thirty move together as a group through space.

*This cluster is the Hickson Compact Group 87 (HCG 87). It includes the spiral galaxy, HCG 87a (lower left); the bright elliptical galaxy, HCG 87b (lower right); the spiral galaxy, HCG 87c (upper center); and the smaller spiral galaxy, HCG 87d (center), which is farther away than the others and may not be a part of the group.*

In terms of the massive size of the universe, the Local Group is only one small part. The Virgo Cluster lies approximately 60 billion light-years away. This *supercluster* is made up of two thousand galaxies. In January 2001, astronomers announced the discovery of another supercluster of galaxies, approximately 6.5 billion light-years away. Made up of billions of stars, this supercluster is now thought to be the largest known object in the universe.

*This spiral galaxy, M100, is located within the Virgo Cluster, a super-cluster billions of light-years away. Newer cameras, such as the one that took this picture, have allowed astronomers to measure individual stars in the Virgo Cluster. This has helped them gain a better understanding of the size of the universe.*

# M100

*A Spiral Galaxy in the Virgo Cluster*

Hubble Space Telescope
Wide Field Planetary Camera 2

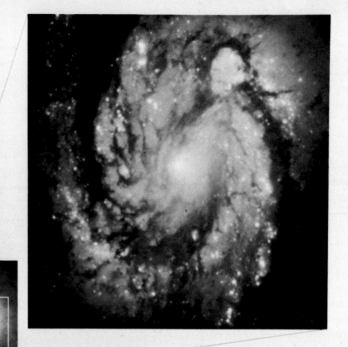

Upper panel shows the nucleus of M100 imaged with the Planetary Camera at full resolution.

Image at left shows a mosaic of the three Wide Field Cameras plus the Planetary Camera.

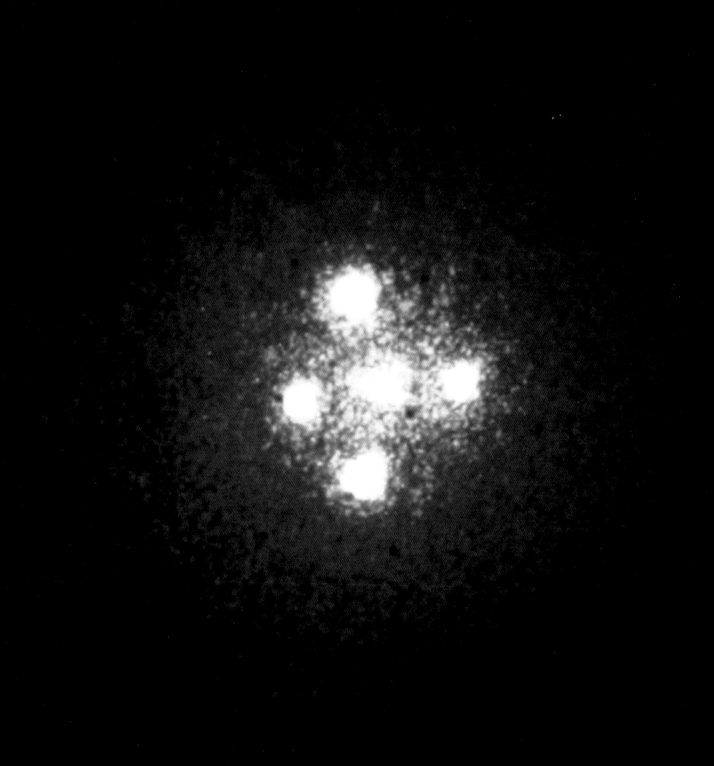

# Quasars

In 1963 Maartin Schmidt, an astronomer living in California, was examining light from a faint blue starlike object. He soon realized that it was giving off one hundred times more energy than our entire galaxy. Even more, the object was no bigger than our Solar System. Recently, astronomers have learned much more about these objects.

*Quasars* were once thought to be bright energy sources located in the centers of distant galaxies that could shine with the light of a trillion suns. Some astronomers now believe that quasars are actually young galaxies whose bright centers are powered by *black holes*.

*The famous Einstein Cross is a phenomenon in which a single object, in this case a quasar, is seen four times. It is named after Albert Einstein (1879-1955), the renowned physicist who predicted the phenomenon in his theory of general relativity.*

A black hole is a region of space that has so much mass that there is no way for a nearby object to escape the pull of its gravity. Some astronomers believe that holes at the center of quasars are continually pulling in and ripping apart nearby stars. However, other astronomers have a different view. They think that quasars are fast-moving objects much closer to Earth.

*This artwork of a black hole shows a glowing disk around a dark center. This disk is formed as matter is pulled by gravity toward the center. The disk glows because it is packed tightly together and heated. Black holes have so much mass and their gravity is so strong that even light cannot escape from them.*

# Are We Alone?

Until recently, the search for life in the universe centered on the eight other planets in our Solar System. But now we know that our Sun is only one of 200 billion stars in the Milky Way and our galaxy is just one of a billion others. So, the question "Are we alone?" takes on new meaning. Some scientists think it is possible that far, far away there is a star with a planet like Earth. Others are not so sure. In January 2000, astronomers Donald C. Brownlee and Peter D. Ward published *Rare Earth: Why Complex Life is Uncommon in the Universe*, in which they suggested that we probably are alone.

*Astronomers Donald C. Brownlee (left) and Peter D. Ward (right) believe that Earth is the only one of its kind in the universe.*

To prove their case, they carefully laid out the conditions that make life on Earth possible.

- Earth is the perfect distance from the Sun so that the planet will not be too hot or too cold.
- The Sun is the right *mass* to ensure that all nine planets will maintain steady orbits.
- Earth has the right amount of oceans and just the right amount of carbon to support life.
- Jupiter is perfectly placed to block any dangerous comets and asteroids.

For these and other reasons, Brownlee and Ward think that Earth might well be one of a kind. Even so, it is hard not to suspect otherwise. With so many unexplored galaxies moving through the universe, astronomers certainly will not run out of places to look!

*This view of Earth was taken from the space shuttle* Discovery. ▶

# Glossary

**Andromeda**—A large spiral galaxy in the Northern Hemisphere 2.3 million light-years from Earth.

**astronomers**—Scientists who study the universe.

**barred spiral galaxy**—A galaxy with a bar of stars that run across the middle.

**Big Bang**—The event around 15 billion years ago that most astronomers believe created the universe. After a giant explosion, matter cooled, separated into large clumps, and formed into systems of stars, dust, and gas called galaxies.

**black hole**—A region of space that has so much mass that there is no way for a nearby object to escape the pull of its gravity.

**cluster**—A group of galaxies that move together through space.

**diameter**—The length of a straight line through the center of an object.

**elliptical galaxy**—A large galaxy that is shaped like a football and contains little dust or gas.

**galaxy**—A system of stars, gas, and dust in space that is held together by gravity.

**gravity**—The natural force of attraction that exists between any two objects.

**irregular galaxy**—A galaxy with no set pattern or structure.

**Large Magellanic Cloud**—An irregular galaxy in the Southern Hemisphere 169,000 light-years from Earth.

**lenticular galaxies**—Galaxies that are shaped like a lens and contain large amounts of dust but not much gas.

**light-year**—The distance light travels in a year. It is a common way to refer to distances in the universe.

**Local Group**—A group of around thirty galaxies, including the Milky Way, that move through space together.

**mass**—The amount of matter in an object, but not its weight. It is a measure of an object or body's inertia, which causes it to have weight in a gravitational field.

**Milky Way**—Earth's home galaxy.

**nebulae**—Clouds of dust and gas in space.

**observatory**—A scientific laboratory devoted to studying the universe.

**orbit**—A full rotation of one body around another. The Earth is in orbit around the Sun. The Moon is in orbit around Earth.

**quasars**—Celestial objects that resemble stars but are much brighter and produce radiation. Once thought to be bright energy sources located in distant galaxies, some astronomers now believe they are young galaxies powered by black holes; other astronomers believe they are fast-moving objects much closer to Earth.

**Small Magellanic Cloud**—An irregular galaxy in the Southern Hemisphere 210,000 light-years from Earth.

**spiral galaxy**—A galaxy with a bulge at the center, surrounded by spirals of stars.

**supercluster**—A giant group of galaxies that move together through space.

# Find Out More

**Books**

Atkinson, Stuart. *Journey into Space*. New York: Viking Penguin Inc., 1988.

Becklake, Sue. *Space: Stars, Planets and Spacecraft*. New York: DK, 1991.

Croswell, Ken. *The Alchemy of the Heavens, Searching for Meaning in the Milky Way*. New York: Doubleday, 1995.

Davis, Kenneth. *Don't Know Much About the Universe*. New York: HarperCollins, 2001.

Lippincott, Kristen. *Astronomy*. New York: DK, 2000.

Parker, Barry. *Colliding Galaxies*. New York: Plenum Publishing, 1990.

Redfern, Martin. *The Kingfisher Young People's Book of Space*. New York: Kingfisher, 1998.

Simon, Seymour. *Stars*. New York: William Morrow and Company, Inc., 1986.

**Web Sites**

Edwin Hubble
www.edwinhubble.com/
www.time.com/time/time100/scientist/profile/hubble.html

General Information on Galaxies
www.damtp.cam.ac.uk/user/gr/public/gal_home.html
www.galaxies.com
www.telescope.org/btl/sg.html

The Milky Way
www.pbs.org/milkyway
www.seds.org/messier/more/mw.html

The Nine Planets
www.seds.lpl.arizona.edu/billa/tnp/nineplanets.html

## About the Author

Dan Elish has written many fiction and nonfiction books for children, including *The Trail of Tears: The Story of the Cherokee Removal*, hailed as an "excellent resource" by *School Library Journal*. He also wrote *Born Too Short, The Confessions of an 8th Grade Basket Case*, which was picked as a Book for the Teen Age in 2003 by the New York Public Library and won a 2004 International Reading Association Students' Choice Award. In addition to that, Dan is an accomplished scriptwriter for television. He lives in New York City with his wife and daughter.

47

# Index

Page numbers for illustrations are in **boldface.**

Andromeda, **28**, 29, 33
asteroid belt, **12**, 13
astronomers
    ancient Greek, 6, **7**
    contemporary, 17–19,
      **19**, 22–23, 25, 29,
      34, 37, **40**, 41–42
    medieval Persian, 29
    in Renaissance, 6, **7**,
      14, **15**

Big Bang theory, **4**, 5
black holes, 37–38, **39**

collisions, 22, **27**
comets, 42

Eagle Nebula, **16**, 17
Earth
    galaxies visible from,
      **24**, **28**, 29–33, **31**
    and Sun, 6, **12**, 14, **15**
    viewed from Space, **43**
Einstein Cross, **36**, 37

galaxies
    barred spiral, 25
    clusters, **32**, 33–34, **35**
    elliptical, 22, **23**, **32**
    irregular, 25
    lenticular, 25
    movement, 26, **27**, 33
    number of, 6, 17–18, 29
    sizes, 9, 22, 30
    spiral, **20**, 21, **28**, 29,
      **32**, **35**
    superclusters, 34, **35**
gravity, 5, 38

Hubble, Edwin, 18–26,
    **19**, 29

Jupiter, **12**, 13, 14, 42

Large Magellanic Cloud,
    30, **31**, 33
light-years, 9

The Milky Way, 10, **11**,
    **12**, 14, 17, 21, 33, 41

nebulae, **16**, 17, 21, **24**,
    25, **31**

orbits, 6, 10, **12**, 14

planets, 10, **12**, 13

quasars, **36**, 37–38

recent discoveries, 34

Small Magellanic Cloud,
    **24**, 30, 33
Solar System, **12**, 13, 14, **15**
stars, 5, 6, 10, 14, 29, 38, 41
    formation of, **16**, 17,
      21, 22
Sun, 5, 6, 10, **12**, **15**, 41, 42

Tarantula, **31**
telescopes, 14, 18, **19**
    images, **16**, **23**

universe, **4**, 5, 26, 34

Virgo Cluster, 34, **35**